The Saga of Aslak

The Saga of Aslak

Susan Price

Illustrated by Barry Wilkinson

A & C Black · London

FLASHBACKS

A Candle in the Dark · Adèle Geras
All the Gold in the World · Robert Leeson
A Ghost-Light in the Attic · Pat Thomson

Published 1995 by A & C Black (Publishers) Ltd
35 Bedford Row, London WC1R 4JH

Text copyright © 1995 Susan Price
Illustrations copyright © 1995 Barry Wilkinson

ISBN 0-7136-4076-6

A CIP catalogue record for this book
is available from the British Library.

Photoset in Linotron Palatino by
Rowland Phototypesetting Ltd,
Bury St Edmunds, Suffolk

Printed in Great Britain by
St Edmundsbury Press Ltd,
Bury St Edmunds, Suffolk

Contents

1	Astrid and Aslak	7
2	Hedeby	17
3	Astrid is Found	26
4	Ejulf	41
5	Ejulfssted	46
6	Odindisa Walks	64
7	The Burial	73
	Further Reading	88

· 1 ·

Astrid and Aslak

There was a man named Ottar Olafssen, who farmed in West Norway. He and his wife, Thora, had three sons and two daughters. Between planting and harvest, Ottar used to go viking. One year he brought home a Saxon slave woman. Ottar was much taken with her, and by her had a daughter, whom he named Astrid, and a son whom he called Aslak.

Their mother, the Saxon woman, soon died. Thora had never treated her well, but after her death, she was kind enough to Astrid and Aslak. It wasn't the children's fault, Thora said, that their father loved foreign slaves.

While Aslak was still small, Ottar set him on his knee before his household, declared that he was his father, and that he set him free. Later he took him to the Assembly and declared his freedom there too. So Aslak grew up free; but Ottar never adopted him into the family, which meant that Aslak would have no right to any of the farm after Ottar died. The land would already have to be shared between Ottar's three sons by Thora. Ottar didn't want trouble in his family.

Nor did Ottar ever free Astrid, because he didn't want to provide her with a marriage-dowry. He already had to provide for his two legitimate daughters. But Astrid enjoyed a comfortable life at Ottarsted, and Thora taught her to spin and weave, to cook and brew, and all the hundreds of things a woman had to know in order to manage a big household well. It was Ottar and Thora's hope that she might find a place as a housekeeper.

Astrid and Aslak looked much alike, and were good friends. They slept side by side and often lay talking late. Astrid was a good storyteller, and would tell Aslak stories most nights.

When Aslak was nine, Ottar sent him to live with a well-respected neighbour, Ketil Law-sayer. Every year, when everyone in the district met at the Assembly, Ketil recited the laws, from memory, so that everyone could hear them. Ottar intended that Aslak should learn the law, to give him a living when he was grown.

Ketil's steding was too far away for Aslak to
come home often. Astrid missed her little brother
badly, and often cried for him at night.

For a time Aslak missed his home, but his big
sister and her stories most of all. He got over it,
because Ketil and his wife Gunnvor were kindly
people. Aslak was bright, and readily learned his
lessons. Ketil would recite them to him in the

mornings, after breakfast, and in the evening. The rest of the time Aslak helped with the farmwork. Ketil would often come up and test him with questions.

Ketil's oldest son, Thord, gave Aslak an axe, and taught him to use it. 'Knowing the law is good,' Thord said, 'but knowing how to defend yourself is better.' Thord was married and settled down, but he had been viking, and would often tell Aslak about his voyages.

Ketil's steding overlooked a fjord, and Ketil owned a boat, for fishing. Aslak loved sailing and, as he grew older, often thought about going viking. He could earn more silver, fame and respect by voyaging that he could as a lawyer. He also thought it a more exciting life than any he could have at home. He talked it over with Ketil and Thord. 'No one can take away from you the law you've learned,' Ketil said. 'It will always be useful. If you want to go viking, I'm not against it.'

When Aslak was fourteen, he got the chance to buy into a trading fellowship. All the members of the ship's crew would put their silver together to buy a cargo; and when the cargo was sold, they would share the profit. Aslak was keen, and rode home to beg his father Ottar for the silver he needed. Ottar was unwilling, because it was expensive, but Aslak said, 'I'm a grown man and my mind's made up. If you won't give me the silver, I shall go as a deckhand.'

Ottar was ashamed that a son of his should work as nothing more than a deckhand, so he asked his other sons if they minded him giving Aslak some silver. They talked it over, and said it was a good idea to make Aslak independent. Then they wouldn't always have to be helping him out later on. So Ottar fetched his scales and weighed out the silver Aslak wanted. He broke an arm-ring to make up the amount.

Before Aslak left, Astrid gave him a silver amulet, a Thor's hammer on a silver chain, to wear round his neck. 'Our father gave me this, but you need it more than me,' she said. 'If you're in need, sell it.'

'Never!' he said.

'Sell it and come home safely rather than keep it and come to harm.' She stood on tip-toe to kiss his cheek. 'Little brother. May Thor watch over you.'

She was afraid that she would never see him again.

Aslak bought a share in the *Brine Stallion*. The crew were sworn to be brothers to each other. All of them had a token, a slice of wood branded with the rune *M*, which meant horse. By showing the token they could get help from other sailors.

They sailed north, and bought furs, and walrus-hide ropes and walrus-ivory; and then they sailed the stormy waters around the coast of Norway to the great market of Kaupang, where they traded their goods for slaves, silks and other things. It was hard work, and Aslak came home stronger, full of tales, and with a little silver of his own. He brought Astrid an amulet to replace hers, though it was only bronze, not silver.

'Have the silver one back, and I'll keep this,' he said.

'I won't take back what I gave.'

'When I have enough,' said Aslak, 'I shall buy you and make you free.'

'Oh, I'm as good as free now.' And certainly Astrid was free in her father's house. She wore coloured clothes on special occasions, and brooches at her shoulders, and a stranger might not have guessed she was a slave.

After that, Aslak went viking each year. He did well, but had to pay his father back, and keep enough silver for the next year's voyage, so he wasn't rich. But he wore silver on each arm, so people knew he was prospering.

At sixteen he was a handsome lad, tall and strong with a fine head of hair; but folk remembered his mother, and called him 'Slave-born'. That year he came home in late summer, and found that his father had died. His half-brothers had divided the property among them. The eldest had kept the farm, but had sold a great deal, to give the others their share in silver. One of the things sold had been Astrid. Being skilled, she had fetched a good price.

'You had no right to sell my sister behind my back!' Aslak said. 'You know if I'd been here, I would never have let you do it!'

'You weren't here,' said his brother, 'and we didn't know if you would ever come back. She was our slave. You know the law – we were within our rights.'

'She was my sister!'

'We needed the silver. I had to sell everything I could, and I still owe our brothers. What could I do? Anyway, she won't be treated badly – I got too high a price for her.'

'Who bought her?' Aslak demanded. He was hoping that it had been some local farmer. Then he could go and buy her back. But his brother told him that, to get the best price, they had gone to Kaupang, and sold Astrid there.

Aslak was so angry, he had to go outside and walk round before he could speak sensibly. Then he went inside and said, 'I want just one thing from you – the name of the man who bought her.'

'He was a trader out of Hedeby . . . A tall man . . . Ragnar, his name was.'

'For this I shall never forgive you,' Aslak said.

He collected his belongings and left his brother's house for good. He rode to Ketil Law-sayer's house, and got Ketil to take him by boat to the home of one of his ship-fellows, Thorgeir.

Thorgeir heard his story and said, 'If we're to find Astrid, we must move fast.' It was late in the year for voyaging, but they found a ship that was sailing east. After making land, they bought horses and rode to Kaupang. There, on the wide meadow sloping down to the sea, were the booths that the traders roofed with oil cloth and lived in while the market was on. Now most booths were roofless and deserted, with only rubbish heaps to show how crowded the market had been.

Aslak and Thorgeir questioned the few traders still there, and they were told of a Ragnar Tokessen, a Dane and slave-trader, from the town of Hedeby.

'I know him,' Thorgeir said. 'He often buys slaves at Kaupang.' And he asked: 'Had this Ragnar bought a girl, a skilled, pretty girl named Astrid?' The traders shook their heads. They hadn't noticed.

'It's as likely a trail to follow as any,' Thorgeir said. 'Your sister is pretty and skilled, you say – then if Ragnar saw her, he would buy her. And he'd sell her in Hedeby, where he'd get the best price.'

Aslak agreed. 'But you should go home. I'm grateful for you coming this far. Astrid's my sister. I'll go on to Hedeby, by myself.'

'We swore fellowship,' Thorgeir said. 'I've come this far – I might as well go the rest of the way. It's dangerous to travel alone – and you haven't the sense of a sheep! Besides, I want to see this pretty sister of yours!'

· 2 ·

Hedeby

Aslak and Thorgeir got a passage on a Danish ship. The captain was sailing home to his steding in Jutland, in North Denmark. Aslak and Thorgeir spent the winter with him there, helping with winter work of repairing buildings and tools. When spring came they took the road that ran the length of Jutland, down to Hedeby. Nothing worth mentioning happened until they got there.

At this time Hedeby was the north's greatest trading town. Its harbour was safe, and thick earthen walls protected it on the landward side. They saw the cloud of smoke from Hedeby's fires at a distance, and Thorgeir said, 'A good cooked meal and a night under a roof!'

They entered by the northern gate, with many others. Those with goods to sell had to pay a tax to guards before they were allowed through. Inside the walls was a wide open space, where traders set up stalls. Many were there already, though it was early in the season. Aslak started looking for Astrid at once. 'She'll be sold by now,' Thorgeir said. 'Let's find lodgings and something to eat!'

Aslak wouldn't listen, but wandered through the stalls. Some were spread with sacks of spices from the far south, others with pots and glassware from the Rhineland. Stalls were stacked with iron ingots or piled with furs. Here and there were the traders' tents, with cooking fires burning before them. Thorgeir and Aslak's mouths watered at the smell of food.

Live animals were squealing as they waited to be butchered or sold; and eggs and cheeses and blocks of salted butter were for sale. Baskets of fresh, dried and salted fish; jewellery and spear-heads; swords – and the Norwegian ships hadn't yet come in, bringing their walrus-hide ropes, furs, walrus-ivory and soapstone bowls. Nor had the ships from England, with their woollen goods, dogs and beautiful metal-work.

There were many slaves for sale, but Astrid was not among them. So they went into town.

The houses were built on the banks of a stream that flowed into the sea. None were big, but they were well-built and comfortable. Only their gable-ends were towards the street, for privacy, and each had a fenced yard. Some had outhouses and even wells. Hedeby was so rich that the streets had walkways of timber, instead of mud and puddles.

The banks of the stream had been faced with timber piles to keep it from flooding and to make it easier to fetch water. This stream was a great convenience. Hedeby, in those days, was a fine town.

After a night's sleep under a roof, Thorgeir and Aslak walked about the market, talking to the stall-holders and asking about Ragnar Tokessen. He hadn't come to market yet, they were told, but he was bound to, unless he'd died.

So they waited. Lodgings being expensive, they went to the harbour, and showed the ship-men their tokens. A trader was always glad to have two more strong young men in his company, in case of attack, and they were given places by the campfires, and food, in return for helping to unload goods. Then one of the sailors told them that Ragnar Tokessen had come.

They found him near the cemetery with a string of slaves, men and women, tied with ropes. Buyers were feeling their arms and legs and checking their teeth. Aslak looked all the slaves over, but Astrid wasn't there. So he started towards Ragnar.

Thorgeir held him back. 'Let me talk to him. You'll lose your temper.'

Aslak nodded. Thorgeir spoke pleasantly, smiling, to Ragnar. 'You're a busy man, I can see, but we have some important business to talk over with you. Could we buy you a drink?'

Ragnar had a trusted slave, Ulf, who managed the other slaves for him. Leaving Ulf in charge, he went with Thorgeir and Aslak to a booth nearby, which sold ale and milk. It was a fine day, windy but sunny, and Aslak sat on the ground while the others sat on a couple of unopened barrels. Thorgeir asked Ragnar about business, and the man answered pleasantly, though warily. 'You weren't at Kaupang last season, by any chance?' Thorgeir asked.

'I was,' Ragnar said. 'And I can tell you two are Norwegians. What's this important business?'

'There may be a little profit in it,' Thorgeir said, smiling. 'Did you buy any women there?'

'I buy women all the time.'

'You bought my sister,' Aslak said. Thorgeir signalled him to be quiet.

Ragnar stared. 'Your sister was sold as a slave?'

'She's committed no crime,' Thorgeir said quickly. 'Aslak's father freed him, but not his sister, that's all.'

Ragnar wasn't happy. 'I know nothing about your sister. I buy and sell women all the time, lads. How can I remember one out of dozens?'

'She had a bronze hammer round her neck,' Aslak said. 'Unless my brother sold that too. She looked like me. She baked, brewed, spun – everything. You gave him a good price, my brother said.'

Ragnar shook his head. 'I can't help you. I must get back.' Nothing would persuade him to stay or say more.

Thorgeir said to Aslak, 'If you'd kept your mouth shut, I'd have got it out of him.'

'Why wouldn't he tell us?' Aslak said.

'He doesn't want trouble! Soon as you opened your mouth he knew you were trouble. You're a fool, Aslak. In future, let me do the talking.'

That evening they were sitting by a fire, eating a good meal of sausage, bread, and dried fish spread with butter, when a man came asking for 'the Norwegians who're looking for the slave girl'. It was Ulf, Ragnar's slave.

Thorgeir and Aslak stepped away from the fire with him, and he asked them, 'Is the girl you're looking for named Astrid?'

'Yes!' Aslak said.

In the firelight, Ulf grinned. 'I remember *her*.'

'She's this man's sister,' Thorgeir said. 'Watch what you say.'

Ulf looked at Aslak. 'You're slave-born, eh? What will you give me to tell you where she is?'

'Do you want to know what I'll give you if you don't tell me?' Aslak asked.

Thorgeir got between them, and said, 'How much do you want?'

'Three ounces of silver.'

'Three!' Aslak said. Thorgeir pushed him further off.

'That's too much. I'll tell you why,' Thorgeir said. 'We must take what you say on trust. You can't expect us to pay three, when you might be setting us to chase the wind. I'll give you an ounce.'

'It's the truth!' Ulf said. 'She was a tall girl – looked like the lad there – had a bronze hammer her brother had given her. Isn't that the truth?'

'Ragnar told you that,' Thorgeir said.

Aslak said, 'Not that I gave her the hammer. We didn't tell Ragnar that.'

'So we know he's seen Astrid. We can't be sure that he knows where she is now.' Thorgeir turned to Ulf. 'Tell me quickly where she is, and I'll give you an ounce and a half. Otherwise, clear off. I'll give you nothing.'

'We sold her to a man named Asvedssen,' Ulf said. 'He lives to the north-east – not far.'

So they borrowed a set of scales from the trader and paid Ulf his ounce and half of silver. He went off happily.

Thorgeir and Aslak spent the evening finding out all they could about the land to the north-east. They bought dried fish and bread to carry with them. Early next morning, they left Hedeby. There's nothing worth telling of their journey until they reached Asvedssen's farmstead.

· 3 ·

Astrid is Found

Men were working the fields at Asvedssted. They saw Thorgeir and Aslak coming, left their work and went to meet them.

The house at Asvedssted was big and old, with straight timber sides and a thatched roof. There were sheds for animals, all well kept. As Thorgeir and Aslak reached the yard, five men were waiting for them, all armed with hoes, axes or picks. A short, grey-haired man was at the front, holding an axe.

Thorgeir said, 'Aslak, keep your temper and keep your mouth shut.'

Behind the men, clustered at the house door, were several women. Aslak suddenly shouted, 'Astrid!' and made to run towards her. Thorgeir dragged him back by one arm, which was good, because the farm men were alarmed.

Thorgeir smiled and said, 'Good day! Are you Manne Asvedssen, Master?'

The grey-haired man nodded. 'Who are you? You aren't Danes.'

'We're traders, from Norway,' Thorgeir said. 'We've come to buy from you.'

Asvedssen was suspicious, but invited them inside, so long as they left their weapons outside. Aslak and Thorgeir didn't like that, but Aslak left his axe, and Thorgeir his sword, and they went in. The farm men crowded in behind them.

The floor was stone-paved just inside the door, and they were asked to leave their muddy boots there. In the rest of the house the floor was hard-stamped earth, spread with straw and herbs.

The main room was panelled in wood and brightly lit. The light came from the fire in its stone box at the room's centre, and from soapstone oil lamps. The broad benches on which people sat and slept were piled with furs, cushions and coverings.

'A fine, comfortable house,' Thorgeir said.

Asvedssen waved Thorgeir and Aslak to their places on the guest-bench, and took his seat opposite them, between the house-trees. The farm men stood in the doorway. Aslak saw that there were weapons on the walls, easily within the men's reach.

Asvedssen's wife had shooed all the women behind a hanging which divided the long room into two. 'A good harvest?' Thorgeir asked the men, and they chatted a while.

Asvedssen's wife returned, with a towel over her arm and carrying a bowl of water, for the guests to wash their hands. Behind her came a young married women, carrying a little ornamented tub, with a ladle; and at her elbow was Astrid, with a tray of wooden cups. Behind her another girl – unmarried, because her hair hung loose – carried a wooden tray of bread and dried fish. When their hands were washed, the young wife ladled drink into their cups, and they said, 'Good health!' and drank. It was mead.

'The best I've ever drunk, Mistress,' Thorgeir said, and nodded to Asveddssen. 'I see you were wise, and found a good housekeeper, Master.'

Asvedssen smiled a little. The men at the door sat on the ends of the benches, and the women took them mead and food too. Astrid and Aslak kept looking at each other.

'So, what do I have that you want?' Asvedssen asked.

Thorgeir said, 'We're traders, so we understand the price of things, and we're always willing to pay fairly.'

'Glad to hear it,' Asvedssen said. 'But what do you want to buy?'

'Slaves,' Thorgeir said. 'There's always a market for slaves. We'll pay a good price. Do you have any you want to sell?'

Asvedssen leaned his elbows on his knees.

'You're joking with me, lads. Hedeby's just a few miles away, and you come here to buy slaves? Come on. Tell me what this is about.'

'Your slave girl there.' Thorgeir nodded towards Astrid. 'Whatever you paid for her, we'll better it.'

'I bought her to help my wife, and very good she is. Besides, she's got a child in her, so I'd be a fool to sell. You don't sell a cow in calf, do you?'

Aslak and Astrid looked at each other.

Asvedssen's wife said, 'Why are you so interested in Astrid?'

'The child is mine,' Thorgeir said. If Thorgeir had been telling the truth, Asvedssen would have had to sell him Astrid – at least, under Norwegian law he would.

'We know whose the child is,' said the wife. 'It's my son's. Manne, they're very keen to buy this girl if they're telling such foolish lies.'

Aslak made to speak, but Thorgeir stopped him. 'I'll be honest with you. I should have been from the start. My friend here is Astrid's brother. She's all the family he has – so you see why he's keen to buy her.'

Everyone looked curiously at Aslak. A man at

the door said, 'You don't look like a slave.'

'I'm not,' Aslak said.

'My friend's father freed him, but not Astrid,' Thorgeir said. 'How about nine ounces of silver, Master? – no, say ten. That's a good price.'

Asvedssen said to Aslak, 'So your mother was a slave?'

Aslak said nothing.

'Huh!' said Asvedssen. *'The child should follow the mother.'*

'What?' said Aslak.

'That's the law, isn't it? Slave mother, slave child. Your father had no business freeing you – we need more slaves, not fewer!'

The farm people laughed. Aslak's face flushed, and he would have risen, but Thorgeir put his hand on his arm.

'A freed slave's no good to himself or anybody!' Asvedssen said. 'If somebody didn't kick him awake, he'd sleep all day! He'll stand all day with a stick in his hand, wondering what to do with it, if nobody tells him!'

Aslak jumped to his feet. 'I know how to use a stick on a lazy, fat Dane without anybody telling me how!'

Thorgeir jumped up too. 'Aslak! Sit down and shut up!' The women cried out and pushed each other behind the hanging. All the men at the door rushed at the strangers. One had grabbed an axe from the wall, and hit Thorgeir on the head with it. Aslak snatched up the mead tub and smacked it in the man's face, and then began laying about him with the ladle. Men were shouting; mead flew everywhere; women were shrieking. There was uproar.

When it was quiet, Thorgeir lay beside the fire, his head bashed in. Aslak was pinned to one of the benches, with four men holding him down.

Asvedssen, looking at Thorgeir, said, 'This one won't live. Take him to the byre, and try not to get too much blood about.'

One of the men holding Aslak said, 'Better to kill this one too. It'll be dangerous to let him go – and he started the fight.'

'Bad enough to have killed one house-guest,' said Asvedssen. 'What did you have to bash him with an axe for?'

Astrid ran up then, and began begging for Aslak's life. She knelt to Asvedssen and said, 'I've worked well for you, haven't I?' She reached her hands towards her baby's father and said, 'Please, please don't kill him; he's just a boy. You gave him food and drink – don't be guilty of killing a house-guest in cold blood.'

The men angrily pushed her away, and her

mistress slapped her and scolded, but she would not be quiet, and they could not withstand her pleading. Asvedssen said, 'Tie him up, and take him to the byre too.'

So Aslak's hands were tied. Astrid stared at Aslak in a way that made Asvedssen lock her in a storeroom, so she couldn't help her brother. Asvedssen was unhappy about what had happened, and didn't know what to do.

Aslak spent the night lying in the byre beside Thorgeir. His ankles had been tied, as well as his wrists. The ropes hurt. His arms and legs became cramped and painful. All the while he could hear his friend breathing in noisy, half-choked gasps. He called Thorgeir's name, but never got an answer. 'Thorgeir, I'm sorry,' he said. Then he couldn't hear Thorgeir breathing any more. 'Don't die, Thorgeir!' For the rest of the night he could feel Thorgeir getting colder and colder, but could do nothing to help.

It was still dark when Asvedssen and his sons came into the byre with a horn lantern. Asvedssen crouched beside Thorgeir, found that he was cold, and said, 'He's dead.'

Aslak knew then that he was friendless, in a

foreign land, and a prisoner among enemies.

Asvedssen rose and said to his sons, 'We have killed a guest.' To Aslak he said: 'Boy, you came and attacked me in my own house. By rights, I should take you to court and get compensation for the injuries you've done me – but I'm not proud of this and I don't want it getting about. Besides, it would take ages and I've better things to do. So I'm going to sell you. Any court would likely enslave you, anyway, so you've no complaint. And it's what you were born to. You might strut about and call yourself free, but you're bone and blood a slave. You'll be happier as one.'

'The trolls take you!' Aslak said.

Asvedssen smacked him in the mouth. 'Well, you'll be happier once you learn to guard that tongue. Listen: I don't want any trouble in Hedeby. Your sister and her child are always going to be here, remember. Make trouble for me, and I'll come back here and make trouble for them.'

Aslak was too angry to speak.

He was untied and stripped of everything: his good hide boots and woollen socks, his red woollen tunic and expensive linen shirt and underdrawers; his leather belt and heavy woollen cloak with its fur lining, and the big bronze brooch that fastened it. They took his arm-bands, and the chains from round his neck. They took his silver Thor's hammer. 'That's Astrid's,' he said. 'Give it to her.'

They laughed at the idea of giving silver to a slave.

'Thieves!' Aslak said. They knocked him down and kicked him.

'Learn to keep quiet!'

He was given an old blanket with a hole cut in it for his head. It hung down to his knees in front and behind, and covered his upper arms, but was open at the sides. Bare-foot, bare-legged, bare-flanked and cold, he was taken back to Hedeby in a wagon.

In the market place in Hedeby a Danish slave-trader called Knud was buying slaves. He looked Aslak over, saw he was young and strong, and said, 'I'll give you six ounces of silver.'

Asvedssen accepted at once. 'I wouldn't sell him, but it's been a tough year and I can't afford to feed him.'

Aslak wanted to say that he was a free man,

but he remembered what the farmer had said about making trouble for Astrid, and he kept quiet.

'I don't care why you're selling him,' Knud said. 'I'm going to Jorvik in Northumbria, and I could sell an old woman on her last legs there.'

All the free men standing around began to ask about the Saxon kingdom of Northumbria, and its capital, Jorvik. Knud told them he had been there a few months ago. The Danish Army were finding it easy pickings, he said. The Saxons had no fight in them. The Danes had taken the Kingdom of the East Angles, and then they'd gone north, across the river Humber, into Northumbria. The Saxons had been holding one of their Christian holidays when the Danes rode into the city of Jorvik, and they'd taken it without a fight!

There was laughter at this. While talking, Knud had been weighing out the silver for Asvedssen. It made Aslak angry to see the silver being handed over to the Danish farmer.

Knud was telling the crowd about the leaders of the Danish army. 'Guthrum's taken Mercia. They say he's going to move into Wessex next. But now Halfdan Wide-Embrace is King of

Northumbria!' There were cheers and laughs from the crowd. 'Aye, the Saxons are well under his heel. He's giving Saxon land to his men, and they're all building good Danish halls on it, and ploughing Saxon earth for Danish seed!' There was more laughter. 'So everybody over there wants slaves – well, you can't make *all* the Saxons slaves, can you? Good business for me! So if anybody wants to sell a slave, come to Knud and get a good price!'

Aslak was taken aboard Knud's ship and roped alongside other slaves in the big hold amidships. He spent several miserable days there before the ship sailed. The ropes rubbed his skin raw, and he was sitting in his own mess. Most of the other slaves were Slavs brought out of Russia. They couldn't speak Norse – but they knew Aslak was Norse and hated him for it. They stole his food; and he was so dispirited about everything that he couldn't be bothered to fight back.

Asvedssen went home and told Astrid to forget her brother. 'Behave yourself and you'll be all right.' Asvedssen's son gave the silver Thor's hammer to his wife. Astrid saw her wearing it every day.

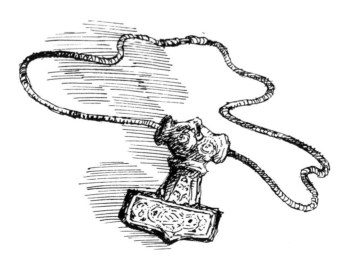

Northumbria

Jorvik

Wales

Mercia

East Anglia

Essex

Wessex

Kent

West Wales

Sussex

· 4 ·

Ejulf

Knud Slave-trader's ship crossed the North Sea and put into Jorvik, in the land of Northumbria. This was in the year 876. Jorvik was not the great trading city it was to become, but many traders and craftsmen from Denmark and Norway were settling there, and it was growing fast. Much of the old Roman fortress, and the old walls, still stood. New quays were being built along the banks of the river, where the fast warships and wide merchant ships tied up.

The Saxons were Christian and had their churches, but the Danes built God-houses for their own Gods. Many new houses were being built. These weren't as fine as the houses in Hedeby, being quickly built of wattle and daub. Nor were the streets clean, but thick with mud and muck. The armed men of the Danish garrison walked through the streets, and the conquered Saxons hung their heads down.

Aslak saw little of Jorvik. The slave ship had met rough seas, and when it reached port, Aslak was weak from hunger and sickness. He hoped and dreaded that, in Jorvik, he might see someone he knew. He was ashamed to be seen as a slave, beaten, tied up and starved. He almost wished he could die, rather than be seen so.

As soon as they tied up at the quay, Knud sent out word that he had slaves for sale, and would be selling them in two days' time. Men came to the quay, clambering on board to peer at the slaves in the hold. Some even came down into the dirt, made the slaves stand, forced open their mouths to see their teeth. Aslak bit a man, and was knocked down. 'A bad temper, that,' said the buyer, and lost interest in Aslak. Knud kicked him, saying, 'Behave!'

On the morning of the sale, the slaves were made to climb onto the quayside and, tied up in ropes, it was hard. The Slavs didn't understand the Danish orders shouted at them and got plenty of kicks and punches.

The selling was brisk, but no one wanted Aslak. Nor did he see anyone he knew.

Among the buyers was a tall, red-haired, red-bearded man. His cloak was of black fur, lined with red wool, and fastened with a big gold pin-brooch. His sword hung from his shoulder on a broad baldric of green cloth sewn with gold thread. He wore round brooches of gold at his shoulders, broad gold bands on his wrists, and a gold ring on every finger. Even his boots were trimmed with glittering braid. It was not a bright day, but he shone with every movement. A band of armed men were with him, wearing helmets and mail coats. This rich man bought several of the strongest Slavs.

Aslak grew tired of standing, and sat. Red-Beard looked at him, but shook his head. 'I need them strong.'

'He's strong,' said Knud. 'A little rest and food is all he needs. He's out of Russia, Jarl, where they breed 'em strong.'

'I am Norwegian,' Aslak said, 'and a free man.'

'Norwegian?' said Red-Beard.

'Yes,' Aslak said, 'like you.'

Red-Beard laughed and nodded. 'What's your name?'

'Aslak Ottarssen, from the West Fjords. Who are you?'

Knud kicked Aslak, but Red-Beard held out his hand to stop him. He said, 'Ejulf Thorhallssen's my name, from Vestfold. Anything else you'd like to know?'

Aslak looked away. 'No. Not unless you're willing to help a free man in trouble.'

Thorhallssen crouched down. 'If you're free, how come you're here?'

'I fell out with a Dane, and he didn't bother to go to law.'

Thorhallssen nodded. 'I'm buying slaves to clear land. This is what I do. I give each slave a piece of land to clear, dung, plough, and get ready for planting. I give them, say, five years to do it. At the end of that time, if the work's done, I free them and let them farm the land. They have to pay rent to me, but they can keep the rest. That way, they work well, so I have less trouble, and the land produces more crops, which is what I need.'

'Why tell me?' Aslak asked.

'Because if I buy you, you'll do your stint like any other man. But in the end you'll be free. Do you agree?'

'I have a score to settle,' Aslak said. 'I can't waste five years farming.'

Thorhallssen laughed. 'I'd hate to leave a West Fjord man with this trader, but I will have what I pay for. If I leave you here, you could be bought by some hard Saxon who'll cripple you to stop you straying and never let you go. So decide. I can't argue with you all day. Do I buy you or not?'

'Buy me,' Aslak said.

So Aslak was sold to Ejulf Thorhallssen, and spent that day, still tied up, locked with the other slaves in an outhouse. The next day Thorhallssen started for his steding, he and his armed men riding, while the slaves walked in line, roped together at the neck.

Thorhallssen rode beside Aslak and asked him for his story. Aslak was still weak, and tired, but over the long journey of two days, Thorhallssen heard it all.

'You really are a free man,' he said, and had Aslak untied. 'But I paid good silver for you and you are still my slave.'

Aslak trudged on without answering. A little while after he began shaking and couldn't stand, and he was put over a horse. When they reached Ejulfssted, he didn't know or care much about it.

· 5 ·

Ejulfssted

Ejulfssted had once belonged to a Saxon, and had been called Oswinssted. Oswin had been killed fighting the Great Danish Army. When the Danes won Northumbria, their leader, Halfdan Wide-Embrance, gave Oswinssted to Ejulf Thorhallssen, as a reward for fighting for him. Now Ejulf punished anyone he heard calling it by its old name. 'I fought for it,' he said. 'Call it by *my* name!'

Ejulfssted was a fine place, built in a fertile valley, wooded with birch and aspen. An earthen wall and ditch enclosed the home-buildings. The hall was of timber, long and high, and roofed with shingles. Before it was a cobbled yard, and standing round were outbuildings: stables, storehouses, cow byres, a smithy. Outside the defences were fields, ploughed and planted. Despite these riches, Ejulf planned to clear more land and make the hall bigger, because he had to keep many slaves, and his family, and a fighting force of ten free men, his housekarls.

Ejulf's wife was named Asa. He had married her in Norway, as a widow. Asa had brought wealth to the marriage as well as two children. There was also a younger brother and sister of Ejulf's. But the most important person at Ejulfssted was his old mother, Odindisa. She was almost sixty, and failing a little; but all her life she had been intelligent and highly-skilled, well able to keep order in her household. She was still handsome, though stooped, and took care with her appearance. Every day she pinned her hair under a linen headdress. Her dress hung from two broad oval brooches which she wore, one on each shoulder. Amber and jet beads were strung between them. The throat of her dress she fastened with a trefoil brooch, and around her waist she wore a belt of silver plaques, from which hung scissors, a knife, and the household keys – for it was Odindisa, not Asa, who said what could be taken from store and what could not. Asa hated this, but Ejulf wouldn't argue with his mother. 'It would be hard for her to give up the keys now,' he said. It was a mark of Odindisa's power that she had a room just for her own use. Not even Ejulf had that.

When Ejulf reached home, it was dark. He had Aslak carried into the hall and laid on one of the sleeping benches, while he saw that the new slaves and the horses were looked after. Then he hurried to the hall, where the tables were being set for the night meal. He was hungry, but before he sat down, he looked round and asked: 'Where's the slave I had brought in here?'

Asa was setting out bowls of water and towels for washing. 'Your mother has him in her room. She's going to look after him.'

'Good!' said Ejulf. He washed his hands, and sat down to his stew and black rye bread.

Odindisa had come into the hall to see everything was straight for her son's homecoming. Seeing Aslak, and how sick he was, she had asked about him. When she heard that he was one of the new slaves, she ordered servants to carry him to her own room. There she had him laid on a straw pallet and covered with a shaggy reindeer hide. She had been putting a cushion under Aslak's head when Asa had come in, to call the servants back to the work she had set them. Asa had said,

'He's still dirty and stinking. He'll spoil all those things.'

Odindisa had answered, 'They are mine to spoil if I please. You could fetch water to wash him instead of standing there whining.'

Asa ordered a servant to fetch the water, and Aslak was stripped and washed. He was hot to touch, but shivered and complained of cold. 'This is bad,' said Odindisa. 'Ejulf may have thrown his silver into a grave.'

Odindisa was learned in medicine, and set about saving the slave for her son. She cut slips of wood, scratched the correct runes on them, and put them in Aslak's bed. She spoke the correct charms; and brewed a bitter drink from willow-bark, which she made Aslak drink. She slept little herself, and whenever Aslak was well enough, by day or night, she fed him bread and broth. When the coughing fits began, she propped him against her shoulder for hours together, and spoke charms, and thumped his back and chest. With the help of the Gods, she saved him, though he was very weak.

Odindisa was pleased with herself, and that made her fond of Aslak. She kept him in her room while he got stronger, and would sit by him, telling him of her life. Three husbands she'd had, marrying the first at thirteen. He'd been much older, and chosen by her father; but once wid-owed, and a wealthy woman, she had chosen her own husbands. She'd had children by all of them, and her family were scattered through Norway, England and the Orkneys. But Ejulf had always been her favourite.

'I haven't much longer in this life. I'm glad to

spend the last of it under Ejulf's roof. I'm making ready for my funeral!' She poked Aslak, laughing. 'I'm choosing the things I want to take with me, and putting by food for my funeral feast. Ejulf has promised me a fine funeral.'

'You'll live many years yet, Mistress,' Aslak said.

'I shan't. And Asa won't be sorry I'm gone. I should like a ship burial . . . But I'm not a queen – though my blood is quite as good as theirs! Maybe Ejulf will make me out a ship in stones. At least he'll raise me a mound, and see that I have all I need.'

As Aslak grew stronger, she asked about his life, and clucked her tongue over it. 'What a sad thing. This life is hard. I often think, the sooner we leave it, the better.'

'Few think that, Mistress!'

'All do, in time.' She heaved herself up, and groaned at her aching bones. 'I'll fetch some broth.'

Once Odindisa was sure that Aslak would live, she wanted her room to herself again. She told him to take his pallet to the hall and sleep there.

The hall was where everyone ate, and slept.

The long walls were almost hidden by the shields and weapons of the housekarls. Their cloaks and furs strewed the sleeping-benches. One end of the hall was curtained off, and Ejulf's family lived behind this curtain. Asa had her loom set up behind it, and there was a closet bed, with doors, built into one corner, for her and Ejulf.

Every day the pallets were rolled up and stowed in a corner, while trestle tables were set up for meals. Every night the tables were taken down, and the pallets unrolled and spread on the sleeping benches again. The housekarls took all the best sleeping places on the benches and nearest the fires, and the slaves had to find space where they could.

Aslak was a newcomer, so he often had to sleep in the entrance hall outside the hall, lying on the stone-paved floor, among the muddy boots of the whole household. The door to the yard was a strong one, in case of attack, but a cold draught blew under it.

Aslak wasn't strong enough to be much use in the fields yet, so he was put to work around the house. Odindisa always sent for him, to run her errands, or just to sit by her and pass her things while she sewed or wove little patterned strips to decorate sleeves and hems. Soon everyone thought he belonged to Odindisa. If Asa saw him, she would say, 'Go and ask Odindisa for something to do.' Aslak didn't like this at all.

He was often sent to the dairy, to fetch Odindisa a cup of milk. The dairy was built on the shady side of the house, away from the heat of the kitchen. When Aslak first saw it, he was impressed by how well-equipped it was. All around the walls were shelves holding big cheeses and blocks of the heavily-salted butter which kept fresh for a long time. Big soapstone bowls and wooden tubs were half-sunk in the floor, and the milk was poured into them. Being half-sunk in the earth helped to keep the milk cool. There were wooden lids to keep dirt out of the milk, and big soapstone ladles to scoop it into the wooden churns. Churning milk into butter was hard work, and Aslak would take a turn at the work, to help the women. He liked going to the dairy, where he could talk to the girls and taste the cream. But if he kept Odindisa waiting long, she would be annoyed. 'I was only away an eye-blink!' he once said. 'You just can't wait for anything.'

Odindisa could hardly believe her ears. She picked up the long wooden rod she used to part the threads on her loom, and whacked it across the palm of her hand. 'If I didn't pity you for having been free, I'd break this across your back, my lad! Now say you're sorry.'

That came hard to Aslak. He gritted his teeth; but remembered that Odindisa had saved his life. 'I am sorry, Mistress. I forgot I am a slave.'

She put the stick down. 'Try harder to remember. And next time I send you to the dairy, spend less time flirting! Don't think I don't know.'

What Aslak hated most was when Odindisa sent him to the kitchens. It happened every day. Asa would send a servant to Odindisa asking for the pantry keys that Odindisa always kept at her belt. Odindisa would send Aslak with the keys, saying, 'Bring them straight back.'

Aslak would go to the kitchen, which was a big, long room, very hot and crowded with busy women. There were fires ringed with flat stones: when these stones were hot, rounds of flat-bread were cooked on them. In the floor were clay-lined pits where the meat was boiled in water heated by hot stones. One woman or another was always working at a quern, grinding grain or peas into flour. What with the quern, and shouting, and iron pots being walloped, it was always noisy. Just by looking into the kitchen you would have known Ejulfssted was a rich man's house – there were more iron cauldrons than were needed, besides roasting-spits, griddles, soapstone bowls, cleavers and buckets of wood and leather.

Asa never took it well when Aslak told her that Odindisa wanted the keys back right away. She would hook the keys onto her belt and go on with as many other jobs as she could find to do.

Aslak didn't mind waiting. While Asa wasn't looking one of the other women would slip him a piece of pickled fish, or ask him to taste the stew or stewed fruit. But he knew that Odindisa would be angry.

The pantry was a big storeroom at the end of the kitchen. When Asa unlocked the door, Aslak would see the big wooden chests inside, holding grain and dried peas. Tall barrels held pickled vegetables, fish and meat. Shelves were stocked with cut cheeses and butter, and precious blocks of salt. From the ceiling hung strings of flat-bread, dried mushrooms and smoked and dried fish that

reminded Aslak of his home in the West Fjords. There were joints of smoked meat, and strings of sausages and blood-puddings that made his mouth water. But Asa kept a strict eye on the stores.

Asa knew where everything was, and how much there was of it. If something was running low, she might send him to fetch more from another storeroom across the yard. It is hard to manage the stores through the year, from one harvest to the next. Rightly is the clever housewife praised!

When she had what she wanted from the pantry, Asa would always say, 'Tell Odindisa I'll give her the keys back this evening. Then I won't have to keep bothering her for them.'

When Aslak told Odindisa that, she would say, 'They are *my* keys. I don't want her leaving them about and letting every little skivvy into the stores. Go and get my keys back at once!'

But when he went back to the kitchen, Asa would find some reason not to give him the keys, and send him back to Odindisa. Often he had to go backwards and forwards between his two mistresses all day.

Once he said to Asa, 'Mistress, if I tell Odindisa she can't have the blasted keys, she'll only send me back again. Why not tell her yourself and save us all a lot of trouble?' He thought he was being helpful, but Asa slapped his face and said she would have him beaten that evening, in the hall, in front of everyone.

Aslak went back to Odindisa with a red mark on his face, and had to tell her what had happened. She got up and went to the kitchen herself, and had a row with Asa that made everyone duck their heads and hide.

Odindisa complained to Ejulf, saying how dared Asa knock *her* property about? Asa complained to Ejulf too, saying she wanted Aslak beaten to teach him manners.

Aslak wasn't beaten, because Odindisa wouldn't allow it. 'When my slaves need beating, *I* beat them,' she said, and Ejulf gave way to her. 'Just as always!' said Asa.

The next time Aslak was slow in running an errand, Odindisa said, 'If ever a slave needed a beating, it's you. But I shan't give you one – to spite Asa!'

Aslak was sick to his heart of being caught

between their silly quarrels. He had dreamed of Astrid, and when he thought that it would take him five years to work off his debt to Ejulf before he could go back to Denmark to find her, he felt desperate. He thought of running away, but he knew that he had little chance of getting far.

So, one day he waited for Ejulf in the entrance, and pulled off his boots for him. He said, 'Jarl, I'm stronger now. I could clear land.'

Ejulf said, 'How's my mother?'

'She hasn't left her bed today.'

'She likes to have you with her.' Ejulf went towards Odindisa's room.

'I need to earn my freedom. I can't spend my time running errands, spinning wool and fetching warm milk!'

Ejulf gave him a look which made him wish he hadn't spoken, and went into his mother's room.

Later, at the evening meal, Ejulf left his place among the housekarls and came and sat at the servant's table, beside Aslak. He said, 'I want you to go on serving my mother.'

Aslak remembered the look Ejulf had given him earlier and kept quiet. It was hard for him to do.

'She's fond of you and likes your company. Very well, I'll count the time you wait on her as time served. Will that suit you?'

'Five years going backwards and forwards to the kitchen?' Aslak demanded.

Ejulf said, 'I've been patient with you because you were a free man. But I bought you, you're my slave, and whatever I order you will do. There's nothing more to be said.'

Ejulf went away. Presently a serving woman came to Aslak and said Odindisa wanted him.

The old lady wanted a cup of milk for her dry mouth. He brought it, and she said, 'Stay and talk.'

'Can I ask you something, Mistress? I want to earn my freedom by clearing land.'

She looked at him over the edge of the cup. 'But Ejulf's given you to me.'

'Oh. But, Mistress – '

'I'm old, so you think me a bore.'

'No, Mistress! – But I am sick of quarrelling with Mistress Asa for you!'

Odindisa was quiet a while. 'You've always been too outspoken, Aslak. A wise man learns to guard his anger and his words. Only a slave speaks as he thinks.'

Aslak had to bite his tongue to keep from giving her an angry answer. 'I didn't mean to offend, Mistress. I'm sorry.'

Odindisa sipped her milk. 'Young men

weren't always in a hurry to be away from me! When I was young, when I wore my hair loose – they buzzed to me like bees to flowers! That was a long time ago.' She sighed. 'Today I asked Ejulf to start making my grave.'

Aslak lifed his head sharply.

'I want to know it's ready. I should like to see it – my everlasting house. I shall be laid in it before the Jul Feast.'

'No!'

'I've looked after many sick people, Aslak. I know. Besides . . . I dreamed . . . Thorlief came to me. My second husband. He stood in this room and said he would soon welcome me to his bed again.' She handed him her empty cup and settled herself against her cushions. 'Four babies and three husbands have gone before me, and I shall be glad to hold them all again. This world is a hard one. I'm not sad to leave it.'

She lay quiet. Aslak thought she slept. Then she said, 'A bargain, Aslak. Work on my grave – Ejulf will be glad of an extra man, he'll want it finished before harvest. Then sit with me in the evenings and tell me the news. How about that?'

'You're good to me, Mistress.'

'I shall be better,' Odindisa said, and he didn't wonder, then, about what she meant.

Odindisa Walks

So Aslak, together with others, worked on Odindisa's grave. Ejulf had ordered it made at a distance, at the edge of the fields. It meant giving up farm land, but he was willing to do that to honour his mother.

The site was cleared by cutting back scrub and burning it off – hot, hurried work as they ran through the smoke beating out flames that threatened to spread further.

But Aslak thought it good to be outside again, even in the rain. At first his muscles ached, but he was long used to hard work and soon got in the way of it again. Every evening he and the others returned hungry to the steding; but he took his meal to Odindisa's room and told her how the work was going.

She would show him what she was taking into the grave with her: a gold and amber necklace; golden bracelets; an ivory comb; spindles, weights, carding combs, needles, scissors, jugs, bowls, linen sheets and woollen blankets. 'Tell me if you think of anything else I'll need.'

'Mistress, any housewife in this world would be envious of these things.'

'Then I shan't shame my husbands. How are the fields?'

'The green is beginning to turn,' Aslak said. When he was hot and sweating, it was a pleasure to straighten and look about while the breeze dried his brow.

'I shan't die before harvest,' Odindisa said, setting her jaw. 'My son won't want to build a grave while there's the harvest to get in.' These days, her face always had a set look, as if she was holding on hard.

One evening she showed Aslak her grave-clothes. The undergarment was of fine wool, dyed blue; and the overdress of scarlet silk. Aslak knew the great cost of that. There were also new boots of calfskin, made by Ejulf's leather-worker. 'I have a long way to go, and these won't wear out on the way,' Odindisa said.

Wood was being felled, and the grave house built; but the fields were also ripening. Soon Aslak and every able-bodied man was put to harvest work. That was hard work. Wagons came to Ejulf's barns, bringing taxes in grain from the farms round about. One day the field workers saw a troop of housekarls ride from the steding, their helmets flashing. No one knew why – but heard later that some Saxon farmers had refused to pay the tax, saying that Ejulf was not the lord appointed by God over them. The housekarls had gone to preach to the Christians a sermon from Odin. Some Saxons were killed, but the rest paid.

'Poor men,' said Odindisa, when Aslak told her. 'My son is right . . . But it must come hard to lose your land and freedom.'

'It does, Mistress,' Aslak said.

She looked at him and said, 'Then come with me.'

'Where Mistress?'

'Into the next world, love. I need a servant, and should like it to be you.'

'I'm a free man!'

'Not yet,' she said. 'Even if Ejulf frees you, you'll be poor and without family. That's hard. Slaves are luckier. Come with me; you'll always have my favour.'

Aslak took a while to answer, thinking hard about his words. 'Mistress, you offer me too great honour. I have things to do, Mistress. I have to fetch my sister.'

'Well,' said the old woman. 'Perhaps I shall take someone else. I daresay old Emma is ready to lay her bones down.'

As Odindisa promised, she outlived the harvest and died with the first frosts. Asa found her dead in bed one morning and went running into the hall where everyone was breakfasting, shouting, 'Oh, Ejulf, your mother's dead, and you were only talking with her last evening!'

People started up, and some women began sorrowful keening. Ejulf went to look at his mother. 'Make her ready for her journey,' he said. 'I'll see that her things are taken to her grave house.'

Aslak was among the men set to carrying goods to the grave house. He was glad to do this last thing for Odindisa. She had been difficult in many ways, but she had also been kind to him, and he was sad that he would never speak to her again in this life.

In the house, Asa and the women stripped the

body and washed it. Asa closed the dead woman's eyes, and bound her mouth closed. Her face was covered with a cloth, and she was dressed in the fine clothes she had chosen for herself. The new boots were put on her feet, and the gold and amber necklace around her neck. The body was laid out on the sleeping bench, and people kept watch over it.

Ejulf set carpenters to erect a bed in the grave house, where Odindisa could lie in dignity. Many men were set to shovelling earth, to raise the mound. And messengers were sent, riding hard, to invite neighbours to the funeral.

'Do you want Saxons at your mother's funeral?' Asa asked.

'We have to live beside them,' Ejulf said.

'We shall show them how things are done,' Asa said, and set slaves to scrubbing, sweeping and finding hangings from chests. Odindisa's keys swung at Asa's belt now. 'Let's hope the bad weather keeps off. We don't want a house full of guests for weeks.'

Candles were always burning near Odindisa's body, and someone was always sitting with her; and yet her spirit walked.

Everyone was in the hall, at the evening meal, when a sudden hush fell. Ejulf looked up, and saw that many people were staring towards the door that led to Odindisa's room. He called out, 'What's the matter?'

No one answered. Ejulf pointed at one man and said, 'You. What's the matter?'

'Nothing, Jarl.'

'Answer me when I ask a question!'

'Jarl – we saw the Mistress look in at the door!'

'Is my wife so terrifying?'

'The old Mistress, Jarl. Odindisa.'

Ejulf left the table and went to Odindisa's room. It was well-lit, and a servant was watching beside the body. He asked if anything had disturbed her, and she said no. Ejulf went back to the hall, and closed the door of Odindisa's room. 'Now no one can look in.' He returned to his meal.

But soon after, men and women started up from their seats, pointing, crying out and jostling. Even the housekarls were alarmed.

Ejulf banged a wooden cup on the table until there was silence. 'You.' He pointed at the same man. 'Now what?'

'Oh Jarl – the old Mistress just looked round the door!'

Several others called out. ' – just the look she used to give us when she was put out – the brooches at her shoulders and the keys at her belt – '

Ejulf bowed his head a moment, then lifted it and called, 'Aslak! Did you see Odindisa?'

'No, Jarl. Not now, not before.'

'Nor I,' said Ejulf, 'but I fear she's come to remind me of a promise I made. Aslak, come with me.'

Aslak followed Ejulf to the door. Ejulf beckoned, and four of his housekarls rose from their places and followed too.

Ejulf led them into Odindisa's room, which smelt of burning candles, herbs and, slightly, of decay. The girl watching by the body would have left, but Ejulf made a sign for her to stay. He said, 'Aslak, you know my mother is to lack for nothing in the next world. You know she needs – '

'I know what you're going to say,' Aslak broke in. 'I don't want to see the Other World yet.'

'I promised my mother you would be her servant. The question is only, will you go willingly?'

Aslak looked at the dead woman, who had been so kind to him. 'This is not the bargain we made, Jarl.'

'I didn't know things would work out like this. But I gave you to my mother – and she comes now and asks me for you. I cannot break this promise, Aslak.' He said to the housekarls, 'I put him in your care. If he doesn't join my mother, you will answer for it.'

As the housekarls dragged Aslak out, Ejulf said, 'It will be quick, I promise.'

Aslak yelled, 'A slave for ever? No!' The housekarls pried his fingers from the doorpost, picked him up and carried him into the yard, to the tackle room, which was strongly built. They tied his hands with rope, and stood guard over him.

He was left to think about dying.

· 7 ·

The Burial

Odindisa didn't walk again. Asa and her women were busy brewing and preparing food for the funeral feast. But it seemed there would be few guests. Some of the neighbouring Danes sent word that they would be coming, but most of the Saxons had sent an excuse.

On the last day of Odindisa's wake, Aslak said to his guard, 'I've been thinking. I've no way out, so this must be the death fated for me. That being so, I'd rather die like a free man, not like a slave or sheep. I'm not a coward. I can die without whining.'

Ejulf was fetched, and when he heard, he said, 'I'd rather you died willingly. It looks better.' But to the guard he said, 'Watch him closely.'

A bier was spread with fine linen, and Odindisa's body lifted onto it. Ejulf, his brother, and some of the housekarls hoisted the bier aloft, and carried it to the grave. Aslak went with them, walking freely, but closely guarded by house-karls. He wasn't thinking of escape. He knew he couldn't get far, and would only make himself ridiculous. Everyone has to die, and better to leave people remembering your courage rather than your fear.

The women were led by Asa, and all carried offerings of meat or bread or mead to place in the grave. As they went they sang the song telling of the road Odindisa had to travel to her new home in the Other World. Aslak listened, thinking of his own journey. And it was while their thoughts were all turned to honouring Odindisa that the Saxons attacked.

The path they followed led round the edges of the fields. People were standing at a distance, wrapped in cloaks, watching. They were people of the district, Saxons, and it was thought they had come out of curiosity to see Odindisa go to her everlasting house. When these people wandered closer, a few of the housekarls became uneasy, reaching for their sword hilts. But Ejulf was thinking only of the funeral and gave no orders.

Coming closer, the strangers shrugged off their cloaks. Then the axes and clubs they carried could be seen. Some even had spears and shields. They yelled and ran to attack.

Those housekarls not carrying the bier drew their swords and tried to surround the women. Ejulf, at first, went on supporting the bier, but as the first weapons clashed, he dropped his side of it and drew his sword. So did every bier carrier. The bier thudded to the ground, and Odindisa's body rolled from it. Her fine grave clothes were muddied.

Aslak found himself unarmed in the middle of a fight, and looked round for a weapon. He saw Ejulf's brother, Olaf, a nice lad, go down with an axe in his neck. Throwing himself on the ground, Aslak reached Olaf's sword. Catching it up, he thrust it into the body of Olaf's killer and rolled away. The sword was almost pulled from his hand before it came free of the wound.

All around was noise. Figures rose up before Aslak and there was no telling whether they were friends or attackers. There was only time to hack at them and hope not to be hurt himself. There was no time to look about, or plan. Only when most of the noise died away, and much of the movement around him stilled could he draw breath and see men running away, and men lying in blood on the ground. The fight seemed over.

He wiped his brow and sat down to get his breath. He had no wounds worth mentioning. The housekarls were wiping blood from their swords and helping those hurt. Aslak watched two kill a Saxon youth, leaving his body lying in the mud as they walked away.

Some serving women were hurt, and sobbing; but the housekarls had done their job and neither Asa nor her children were harmed.

Aslak wandered along what had been the funeral procession. He still carried Olaf's sword. Ejulf was sitting, panting, on the ground while a housekarl pressed a cloak to a wound in his leg.

Aslak held out the sword he carried, and said, 'Olaf's sword, Master. I used it for him, after he went down.'

'Is he hurt?' Ejulf asked.

'He's dead,' said Aslak.

Ejulf set his teeth and gave two short nods. It was easy to see that he was grieved.

'Do you know law?' Aslak asked.

'Is Asa safe?' Ejulf said. 'What about law?'

'I learned law when I was younger. When a slave fights for his master against attackers, that slave is free.' And he quoted the law, just as he had learned it.

Ejulf stared. 'Put my mother's body back on her bier.'

Aslak laid the sword beside Ejulf and went to help with the body.

Ejulf had much to distract him, but he asked his housekarls, 'Did Aslak fight for us?'

One said, 'He killed the man who killed Olaf. I saw that.'

'Then he's free,' Ejulf said. 'My mother must take another slave. She and Olaf will be travelling together.'

Ejulf, his wound tied up, rode out with his housekarls, to hunt down their attackers. He made short work of those he found, to save them the trouble of going to law at the next assembly.

Odindisa was carried back to the steding, and made clean again, and put in a cold outhouse while her son, Olaf, was made ready for his grave. They were laid side by side in the grave house, with all Odindisa's things, and Olaf's armour and sword. His favourite horse was killed and buried beside him, with all its harness. Beside them were laid loaves of bread, joints of meat, and flasks of mead. Ejulf tucked a purse of silver coins into his brother's belt.

An injured slave woman died from her wounds and was put into the grave. Another slave was close to death and was carried to the grave where Ejulf cut his throat, sparing him much pain. Everyone said the slaves were lucky to be getting a burial so much better than their worth.

Aslak helped to raise the earth over the grave house, making a large mound. On top was set a wooden post, and one of the housekarls carved on it, in runes: *This mound was raised by Ejulf, to his mother Odindisa, a lady generous and fair, and to his young brother, Olaf, who had proved himself no coward and a loyal friend.*

Aslak stayed on, because he was not yet legally free. In the spring he rode to the assembly with Ejulf and his housekarls, and there Ejulf announced, before witnesses, that Aslak Ottarssen was a free man. Ejulf gave him a gift of a green tunic, so he would no longer be dressed in grey homespun cloth, like a slave.

Aslak laughed and said, 'My foster father always said knowing law would come in useful.'

Aslak had quoted Norwegian law to Ejulf. But Northumbria was under Danish law. Aslak was glad, because Danish law granted freedom much more quickly and simply. Norwegian law demanded that a freed slave give a freedom feast, and left him under many obligations to his old master. But Danish law said, once freedom had been witnessed, a man was entirely free.

'What will you do?' Ejulf asked, when they sat together in a drinking booth, with Aslak wearing his new green tunic.

'Fetch my sister out of Denmark. She may have a child by now. She's all the family I have.'

'It's dangerous to be without family,' Ejulf said. 'What if I took you into my family?'

'"A gift always looks for a return,"' Aslak said. 'What do you want?'

'I'm not making you my blood brother – only a member of my household. People know what happens when they injure one of my household. And I'd give you a piece of land to clear, and you – '

'Just as when I was a slave!' Aslak said. 'No, I'll tell you what I'd like, Ejulf. I'm a trader. You're rich. Set me up with a ship, and I'll share the profits with you.'

Ejulf chewed his thumbnail. 'This needs thinking about.'

'While Astrid's in Denmark, I can't wait for you to think. Lend me the money to buy into a fellowship.'

Ejulf agreed. So Aslak rode into Jorvik, and sought out Norwegian traders. He found some men who knew him and could swear that he was honest. So he was able to buy into a fellowship. In early summer he sailed for Denmark.

There is not much more to tell. Aslak told his story to his shipmates, and they were angry for him. Several of them agreed to help him when the time came.

The ship put into Hedeby and did good trade. Towards the end of their stay Aslak and his friends rode out fully armed to Asvedssted.

But Astrid was dead. She had died when the child had been born. The Danish farm wife was scared but she looked Aslak in the face and said, 'I did all I could for her. I didn't want her to die. Nothing could have saved her.'

'What of the child?' Aslak asked.

A woman came forward, holding a baby. The farm wife said, 'I gave her to this woman, because she had milk.'

Aslak took the child in his arms and went outside, holding her. He sat down on the bench in front of the house, bowed his head and hugged the child to him.

His friends made the farm-people bring them food. They left Aslak alone because they thought he was weeping.

When he came back into the house he said, 'I want this child. I'll take this woman too, to feed her.' He looked at Asvedssen. 'You killed a friend of mine, and enslaved me. You said you had a right, but it was never put to law. Give me this child and this woman, and I'll take my men away and consider your debt to me paid.'

'Take them,' said Asvedssen. He was afraid of Aslak's friends.

As the ship-fellows were leaving, Aslak turned back with the child in his arms. 'Do you remember taking a silver hammer from me, a Thor's hammer? It belonged to my sister. Do you still have it? If you do, give it to me. I want her daughter to have it.'

One of the farm women was still wearing the hammer, and she quickly took it off and held it out. One of Aslak's ship-fellows took it and hung it around Aslak's neck.

After that the ship-fellows rode back to Hedeby, Aslak carrying the baby and the woman riding behind one of his friends. They soon sailed for Jorvik.

When Aslak got back to Ejulfssted with the baby, Ejulf was pleased for him. Aslak offered him half of his profit, to pay him back part of the silver he had lent him.

'Keep it,' Ejulf said, 'for next year's trading. You really are a trader, Aslak. I shall have to see about that ship.'

Aslak named the baby Astrid after her mother. At first she lived in the hall at Ejulfssted, in the care of the slave woman who had mothered her from birth. But Aslak thought he should have his own house, and Astrid should have a mother. He consulted Ejulf, and Ejulf said, 'Leave it with me.'

A while later Ejulf suggested that Aslak marry a Saxon widow who had a bit of land. Her husband had been killed after the fight at Odindisa's funeral, and she could no longer work her land

and pay tribute to Ejulf. 'Better you working it than some Saxon I can't trust,' Ejulf said.

Aslak said he wouldn't take the widow or the land if it meant Astrid might be in danger. 'Nowhere is safe,' Ejulf said. 'But the Saxons have had the fight knocked out of them. If anything happened to you they'd have to answer to me and my housekarls, and they all know that. I can give you some men to help with the land.'

So Aslak married the widow and raised a fine family with her. They raised Astrid too, and she grew very like her mother, or so Aslak thought. When she was old enough, he took the silver hammer from round his own neck and put it on hers. 'That belonged to your mother,' he told her. 'She was given it by her father, Ottar Olafssen in Norway, and she gave it to me when I went on my first voyage.' And he told her the whole saga of the hammer, and her mother, and how he had lost them both, but had only regained the hammer. Little Astrid often wept for her dead mother, but loved to hear how Aslak had fetched her from the Dane's house.

She grew up a handsome and skilled girl, and married a Dane, one of Ejulf's housekarls. She told the saga of Aslak to her children, and they told it to theirs, and that is how it is known.

In his later years Aslak wasn't called 'Slave-born' any more, but 'Twice-freed', because he'd been freed by Ejulf as well as his father. Ejulf bought him a ship. Aslak named it *Gold Snake*, and made many voyages in her. He shared the profits with Ejulf.

Aslak became wealthy. He raised memorial stones to his sister Astrid, and his ship-brother Thorgeir, and made offerings for their spirits. He hoped to meet them both again when he made his last voyage, out of this world and into the next.

To the end of his days Aslak was a man who spoke his mind, never learning to guard his tongue. His neighbours thought he treated his slaves better than they deserved.

He died old, in Northumbria, and his sons made a grave house for him, and raised a mound over it. His sister's daughter Astrid paid for the outline of a ship to be picked out around the grave in stones, so that he would have a ghost-ship to sail on his ghost-voyage to the Other World.

Here ends the saga of Aslak Slave-born.

Further Reading

Now that you have read **The Saga of Aslak**, you might like to read some other books about the Vikings. You might like to read other novels, or general information books. Here is a selection of the books available.

Fiction

Rosemary Sutcliff **The Shield Ring**
Puffin Books (1992)

Rosemary Sutcliff **Blood Feud**
Puffin Books (1994)

Non-fiction

John D. Clare **Vikings**
(in the **I Was There** series),
The Bodley Head Children's Books,
London (1991)

Susan M. Margeson **Viking** (Eyewitness Guides)
Dorling Kindersley, London (1994)

Hazel Mary Martell **The Vikings**
(in the Young Researcher series)
Heinemann Educational Books,
Oxford (1991)

Marilyn Tolhurst **Viking Street** (in the **What Happened Here?** series)
A & C Black, London (1994)